The Rainbow Bear

For dear Ted,
who taught me how bears shed rainbows,
and so much more besides.
M.M.

The Rainbow Bear

Michael Morpurgo

illustrated by Michael Foreman

Picture Corgi Books

I am snow bear. I am sea bear. I am white bear. I wander far and wide, king in my wild white wilderness.

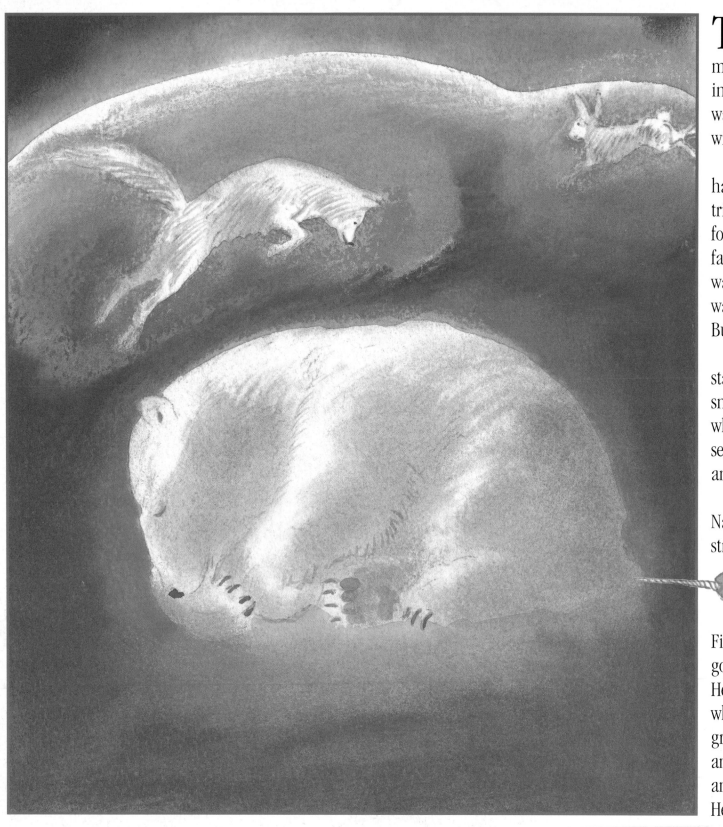

The snow has darkened around me again. I have dug my den deep into the mountainside. Here I am warm. Here I shall dream away the winter...

There will be plenty of hopping hares to pounce on. But hares are tricky. Plenty of frisking foxes. But foxes are fast. Plenty of wallowing walruses. But walruses are big.

Seals are slow. Seals are best. I stalk them silently. Silently. I am snow bear in a world of white and they cannot see me coming. But one sound, and a seal slips away into the sea.

A seal in the sea is slippery quick. Narwhals and beluga whales are strong, too strong.

Fish flash by like silver light and are gone before they were ever there. Here all about me is whooping and whistling of whales. Here is groaning and grinding of ice. Here I am snow bear no more. I am green and blue and indigo and turquoise. Here I am sea bear.

I clamber out of the sea. I
shake myself dry in the sun.
I am snow bear again. I look
about me.

Rainbow! Rainbow over my
wild white wilderness. Beautiful
and bright he was, more
wonderful than anything
I had ever seen before.
I knew at once I had
to catch rainbow
and make him mine.
So I went after him. I
went hunting rainbow.

I leapt from ice floe to ice floe. I galloped through snow. Ever closer, ever closer. I stalked him silently. Silently. And there at last was rainbow, just one leap away. I pounced.

But I pounced on snow, on white white snow. Rainbow was gone, vanished with the wind. I lay in wait for him, for days, for nights, but he never came back. So I went looking for him. I roamed my wild white wilderness. I would hunt nothing but rainbow.

How long I wandered I did not know. I was weary. I was hungry. I knew I must eat, or I would die.

I smelt man. Then I saw man. Man is clever. Man is danger. But this man was alone and I was hungry. This man was sitting on the ice. He was fishing.

I stalked him silently. Silently. When he saw me, he did not try to run. There was no fear in his eyes, only wisdom.

"So, my friend," he said, "so you have come to eat me. I'm old, very old, I'm not much of a meal for a king of a bear like you."

And it was true. He was old, little more than skin and bone. But a meal was a meal. I made ready to pounce.

"Only leave me to live out my days, my friend," he went on, "and I shall grant you your dearest wish. For I am wiser than man. I am shaman. I know all there is to know. I know you hunt rainbow. But rainbow cannot be hunted, cannot be caught. All you can do is let rainbow come to you. And when he does, you must not pounce on him, you must wish on him. Then all you wish will come true. This I promise you."

The wise old shaman turned back to his fishing again.

So I walked off and left him there on the ice. I did just as he had told me. I hunted no more for rainbow, only for seal and fox and hare. But I still looked everywhere for rainbow.

Every night I dreamt of him. Then one morning I woke and rainbow was there. It was him! It was rainbow leaping out over the sea and across the sky towards me. I remembered again the wise old shaman's words. So I sat on my mountainside and waited, and hoped. And waited and hoped. Nearer he came, nearer still, until he stopped right over me. I was soaked through in his colours. I was rainbow too! I knew at once what to wish for.

I closed my eyes and I wished. "Let me only stay like this, just as I am at this moment. Let me be rainbow bear."

When at last I opened my eyes, rainbow had gone from the sky above me. But I was rainbow, rainbow all over! I was rainbow bear!

I cavorted, I frolicked. I tumbled down the mountainside. I rolled in the snow. I plunged into the sea. When I came out I shook myself dry. I was still rainbow bear! No bear before me had ever been happier than I was then.

I went to find the old shaman, to tell him, to show him. It was far to go, so I hunted as I went. I smelt seal. I stalked him silently. Silently. But seal saw me coming and was quickly gone. I smelt fox. I stalked him silently. Silently. But fox saw me coming and was quickly gone. I smelt hare. I stalked him silently. Silently. But hare too saw me coming and was quickly gone.

By the time I found the wise old shaman again, I was weak with hunger.

"Ah, my friend," he said. "Wherever I go they speak of little else but you. Out at sea, the whales whistle and whoop of it. The waves murmur it. At night the snowy owl hoots to the moon of it. And all say the same: 'Have you seen the rainbow bear? Is he not the most beautiful bear the world has ever seen?' And you are. But there is much danger in beauty, my friend."

And even as he spoke, he pointed out to sea. A great ship was stealing towards us through the ice floes, silently. Silently.

"Look!" he cried. "They have come for you, my friend. Run! Hide yourself! Go, before it is too late!"

So I ran and ran, but the men from the great ship came after me with their dogs and their guns. I hid where I could, but wherever I hid they found me. I was no longer a white bear in a white world. I made for my mountainside, for my winter den. But the men soon dug me out. I was too weak to fight the net they threw over me.

"We have him!" they cried. "We have the rainbow bear! Let's take him back to the ship. He'll make us a fortune."

And so they took me away.

Oh, I had everything I had wished for. I was indeed rainbow bear, but my kingdom was now a cage. I could see the moon, I could see the stars — all through the bars of my cage.

In their thousands, they came to stare at me, to laugh at me. My only escape was in my dreams. But when I dreamt it was always of the wild white wilderness I had left behind and would never see again. I would be white bear again, white bear hunting, white bear stalking. But always I woke, and always the bars were still there.

And so my days passed, each day as long as a winter, each day the same – until early one morning when a voice roused me from my dreams.

"Mr Bear," came the voice. "Oh, Mr Rainbow Bear." A small boy was gazing up at me through the bars of my cage.

"I've been watching you, Mr Rainbow Bear," said the boy. "You just sit there and rock. You just walk up and down. You hate it in there. You hate being a rainbow bear, don't you? You're thinking, I want to be like other snow bears, I want to be back home where I belong, in all that ice and snow, with all those seals and walruses."

Suddenly he was up on the wall and pointing at the sky. "Look, Mr Rainbow Bear!" he cried. "Just like you! It's a rainbow, a rainbow! Don't you know, don't you know? Just find the end of a rainbow and you'll have all you could wish for. It's coming closer, closer. It's coming right over us now! We're at the very end of the rainbow. Quick! You wish. I'll wish. We'll both wish together."

He closed his eyes and lifted his hands into the rainbow above us. Now he was rainbow all over, just as I was.

"We wish this bear was white," cried the boy. "We wish this bear could go back home where he belongs, where he'll be happy. Now, this very minute."

And the boy wished, and I wished with him. I wished myself white. I wished myself away, and back home.

I am waking up, waking up. I have been dozing long enough down in my den. Time to get up. Time to hunt. There's the light of spring seeping through the snow above. I'll dig myself out.

Blue, blue sky. Eye-dazzling sun. Wonderful sun. New air. Icy air. I breathe in deep. The long winter sleep is done and forgotten now. How I wish I could remember my dreams. But I never can.

I clamber out. I cavort, I frolic, I tumble down the mountainside. I roll in the snow. I plunge into the sea. It is so good to be alive, so good to be wild.

I am snow bear. I am sea bear. I am white bear. I wander far and wide, king in my wild white wilderness.

THE RAINBOW BEAR
A PICTURE CORGI BOOK : 0 552 546402

First published in Great Britain by Doubleday, a division of Random House Children's Books

PRINTING HISTORY
Doubleday edition published 1999
Picture Corgi edition published 2000

5 7 9 10 8 6

Text copyright © Michael Morpurgo 1999
Illustrations copyright © Michael Foreman 1999

Designed by Ian Butterworth

The right of Michael Morpurgo to be identified as the author and of Michael
Foreman as the illustrator of this work has been asserted in accordance with the
Copyright, Designs and Patents Act 1988

Picture Corgi Books are published by Random House Children's Books,
61-63 Uxbridge Road, London W5 5SA,
a division of The Random House Group Ltd,
in Australia by Random House Australia (Pty) Ltd,
20 Alfred Street, Milsons Point, Sydney, NSW 2061,
in New Zealand by Random House New Zealand Ltd,
18 Poland Road, Glenfield, Auckland 10,
and in South Africa by Random House (Pty) Ltd,
Endulini, 5A Jubilee Road, Parktown 2193

Printed in Singapore